GHOST DETECTORS

All Dolled Up!

BOOK 21

BY
JAN FIELDS

ILLUSTRATED BY
DAVE SHEPHARD

Calico

An Imprint of Magic Wagon
abdopublishing.com

For all the fantastic people who edit my work and make me look so good.— JF

To Kelly, for everything.— DS

abdopublishing.com

Published by Magic Wagon, a division of ABDO, PO Box 398166, Minneapolis, Minnesota 55439. Copyright © 2018 by Abdo Consulting Group, Inc. International copyrights reserved in all countries. No part of this book may be reproduced in any form without written permission from the publisher. Calico™ is a trademark and logo of Magic Wagon.

Printed in the United States of America, North Mankato, Minnesota.
092017
012018

 **THIS BOOK CONTAINS RECYCLED MATERIALS**

Written by Jan Fields
Illustrated by Dave Shephard
Edited by Bridget O'Brien
Designed by Christina Doffing

Publisher's Cataloging-in-Publication Data

Names: Fields, Jan, author. | Shephard, Dave, illustrator.
Title: All dolled up! / by Jan Fields; illustrated by Dave Shephard.
Description: Minneapolis, Minnesota : Magic Wagon, 2018. | Series: Ghost detectors; Book 21
Summary: Pop Quiz Porter invites Malcolm and Dandy to her house to get rid of a ghost haunting her huge collection of creepy dolls.
Identifiers: LCCN 2017946453 | ISBN 9781532131530 (lib.bdg.) | ISBN 9781532131639 (ebook) | ISBN 9781532131684 (Read-to-me ebook)
Subjects: LCSH: Ghost stories--Juvenile fiction. | Best friends--Juvenile fiction. | Dolls--Juvenile fiction. | Humorous Stories--Juvenile fiction.
Classification: DDC [FIC]--dc23
LC record available at https://lccn.loc.gov/2017946453

Contents

Chapter 1
You've Been Invited!

Malcolm dragged his best friend into the yard. Every inch was crammed with stuff from the garage. "Ta-da!"

Dandy, whose real name was Daniel Dee, wiped his nose with his shirt sleeve. "What's with all the junk? Are you having a yard sale?"

"No," Malcolm snapped. "This is the Ghost Detectors training course. It will turn us into lean, mean, ghost hunting machines."

Dandy sniffled and scratched his head. "Like robots?"

Malcolm ignored the question. He liked robots too. But so far he hadn't found a way to combine ghost hunting and robots. "We run, climb, jump, crawl, and slide through the course. Then we'll be better at those things when we chase ghosts."

"I don't remember any sliding."

"You would if we practiced it." He pulled a stopwatch out of his pocket and handed it to Dandy. "Here, you time me. Then I'll time you. That way you can see the whole course."

Dandy stared at the stopwatch in his hand and rubbed at his nose again. "Okay, go!"

Malcolm raced to the ladder and climbed to the top. Then he dangled his legs and

jumped off onto a pile of sleeping bags. He crawled under a row of sawhorses. Finally, he slid across a tarp staked down with his dad's tent stakes.

Malcolm trotted back to Dandy, panting. "How did I do?"

"You looked great." Then he sneezed all over the stopwatch.

"How fast did I go?"

"I don't know." Dandy held up the dripping watch. "I can't read it."

Malcolm sighed. "We'll wash it off, then you can go."

"But I just got here."

"Not go home. Take your turn."

"Hello, boys!"

Malcolm and Dandy turned to see Mail Carrier Nancy pulling her mail cart. She waved and walked toward them on the sidewalk. "I've got something for you."

Malcolm whooped. It must be the Super Chiller Ghost Freezing Spray he had

ordered. He didn't think it would come so fast.

But Mail Carrier Nancy held out a flat envelope. Malcolm frowned. There couldn't be a can of freezing spray in there.

As Mail Carrier Nancy pulled her cart down the sidewalk, Malcolm tore open the envelope. The card inside made him groan.

Dear Malcolm and Dandy,

I heard about what you boys did. Please, come to my house as soon as you get this note! I have a chore for you.

Sincerely,

Ms. Porter

"Is that?" Dandy wiped his nose again.

"It is." It was almost too terrible to think about. Pop Quiz Porter, the oldest and

meanest substitute teacher in the world, wanted them to come to her house.

"She says she knows what we did," Dandy said. "What did we do?"

"I don't know, but it must have been terrible."

Just then, something dark and scary snuck up behind them. A long arm with black fingernails snatched the note out of Malcolm's hand. It belonged to his sister, Cocoa.

She wore a black skirt, tattered black leggings, and high-top black sneakers. His parents said she was going through a phase. With all the gray smudged around her eyes, she looked more like she was going through a horror movie.

"You two are in trouble," she sang out. "Wait until Mom sees this."

"Give it back!" Malcolm shouted. Cocoa just laughed and ran for the house. With her long legs, Malcolm couldn't catch up.

He and Dandy panted like dogs as Cocoa handed over the card to Mom. "Look what came in the mail!"

Mom looked at the card. Malcolm held his breath and waited for the yelling to start. Instead, Mom smiled.

"This is wonderful," she said. "You two must have done something very nice for a teacher to invite you both to her house."

Cocoa crossed her arms. "These two?"

Mom just gave her the stink eye before turning to Malcolm and Dandy. "You boys head over to Ms. Porter's house. I'll call and let her know you're coming."

With no choice, Malcolm and Dandy headed for their bikes, and their doom.

Chapter 2
Meet the Family

Malcolm and Dandy stood on the walk in front of Pop Quiz Porter's house and stared. The house was small and brown with fancy white trim. It looked like a gingerbread house from a fairy tale.

"I feel like Hansel," Malcolm said. "Only I didn't leave any bread crumbs."

"Does that make me Gretel?" Dandy asked. "Because I don't want to be Gretel."

Malcolm huffed at his friend. "Nobody has to be Gretel. But if Pop Quiz Porter

offers us snacks, we should probably pass on them."

"Snacks! What kind of snacks? Now I'm hungry." Dandy grabbed his stomach and groaned.

"Forget the snacks. Let's get this over with." Malcolm rolled his bike up the walk and Dandy followed. Then Malcolm stopped so suddenly that the front wheel of Dandy's bike bumped into him.

"What?" Dandy asked.

Malcolm pointed toward the closest window. Pale, blank faces stared out at them. More faces stared from every window they could see.

"Do you think those are ghosts?" Dandy whispered. "Maybe I don't need snacks."

"Not ghosts," Malcolm whispered back. "They aren't moving."

Dandy sniffled. "Maybe we should go back to your house and practice our Ghost Detector skills. I still don't know how to slide. We could come back later after I know how to slide."

"You might be right. We need the practice." Before Malcolm could turn his bike around, the front door flew open.

Pop Quiz Porter stood in the doorway. Her gray hair hung down to her shoulders. She wore a fluffy sweater with a smiling rag doll on the front and blue jeans.

Malcolm and Dandy both stared at her. Teachers never wore blue jeans. Malcolm was pretty sure it was a law or something.

The teacher opened her arms and smiled. She never smiled at school. It made Malcolm nervous. "Come in, boys. Come in," she said.

That's probably what the witch said too. Malcolm swallowed hard. He thought about running, but his mom would just send him back. He laid down his bike and walked up the steps to the house.

Ms. Porter stepped back to let them pass. Malcolm saw the dolls as soon as he came through the door.

Tall dolls stood along the walls and stared out the windows at the world. Cloth dolls flopped out of baskets on the floor. Troll dolls peered down from shelves. Dolls sat on every piece of furniture and peeked from packed glass cabinets. Three dolls sat on a ragged rocking horse.

"Do you like my family?" Ms. Porter asked.

"You sure have a lot of dolls," Dandy said.

Ms. Porter giggled. "I've always loved dolls. I can't seem to get enough of them."

Malcolm cleared his throat and fidgeted nervously. All the staring eyes were making him nervous. "You said you had a chore for us, Ms. Porter?"

"There's plenty of time to talk about that." The teacher herded them toward the sofa. "You boys sit down, and I'll bring in some tea and cookies."

"Do cookies count as treats?" Dandy whispered.

"Yes."

Malcolm and Dandy wedged in between the dolls already sitting on the sofa. More dolls perched along the back. Malcolm was afraid to move.

"This is the creepiest place we've ever been," he whispered to Dandy.

Dandy rubbed his sleeve across his nose. "Why is she acting so nice? She hasn't yelled at all. It's weird."

"I know," Malcolm agreed. "It's like watching a bomb tick. You know it's going to blow. You just don't know when."

Dandy nodded. Then he sneezed. The dolls on the back of the sofa toppled off onto them.

As Malcolm and Dandy batted them away, the dolls sitting on the ends seemed to fling themselves over onto the boys. More and more dolls tumbled from the shelves onto their heads.

Pale, cold doll faces with bulging eyes and yawning mouths pushed against the boys. Malcolm and Dandy yelled.

Then china doll teeth sunk into Malcolm's ankle. He kicked and the doll

flew through the air and landed in a basket of cloth dolls.

"Ow," Dandy howled. "They're caught in my hair."

Malcolm pulled the doll fingers loose, making Dandy yelp some more. Then Malcolm grabbed a fluffy pillow to beat at the dolls, but more and more piled on.

Soon Malcolm couldn't even see Dandy under a squirming pile of dolls. He could barely hear his friend's muffled screams.

Malcolm heard the clatter of dishes as he dug through the pile looking for Dandy. Ms. Porter carried the tea tray in and put it on a table. The dolls stopped moving.

Dandy's head popped out of the pile of dolls.

Ms. Porter folded her hands in front of her. "I see you've met my ghost."

Chapter 3
Poltergeist Popper

Ms. Porter took a long, noisy sip of her peppermint tea. Then she smiled sweetly at the boys. "I think one of my dear little dolls came with a ghost."

"Which doll?" Malcolm asked.

Malcolm balanced his teacup on his knee. He didn't know if the stinky tea counted as a treat, but he sure didn't want to drink the stuff. Dandy left his cup on the tray and shoveled sugar cubes into his mouth.

The teacher's smile slipped as she watched Dandy. Then she cleared her throat. Dandy didn't stop. "I don't know which doll is haunted," Ms. Porter said. "That's why I need you."

"Why uff?" Dandy asked around his mouthful of sugar.

Her smile slipped some more. "Mrs. Goolsby told me you boys took care of a little ghost problem for her. I need you to do that again. Right away. I find this ghost upsetting."

Dandy sneezed again. He sprayed half-chewed sugar cubes all over.

Malcolm jumped aside, forgetting the teacup on his knee. It splashed tea across the tea set. Malcolm ducked to grab the cup before it could hit the floor. Dandy did the same. The boys smacked their heads

together and the cup hit the fluffy rug on the floor.

Pop Quiz Porter looked at the bits of sugar sticking to her tea set and the puddle of tea on the tray. "I expect you to take care of the ghost without messing up my house."

"Sure," Malcolm agreed. "We just have to go get our gear."

"And an ice bag," Dandy said as he rubbed his head.

The teacher pointed at them. "Make it quick. I'll be staying with Mrs. Goolsby until you get rid of the ghost."

The boys made it quick, at least as far as Malcolm's house. They were still panting as they walked through the door. Cocoa stood in the hall with her hands on her hips.

"How much trouble are you in?" she asked with a smirk.

"None," Malcolm said, crossing his arms over his chest. "We're doing a job."

"Sure you are." Cocoa poked her long nose closer to Dandy and sniffed. "Why do you smell like sugar and peppermint?"

Dandy sniffed the wet hem of his shirt. Then he licked it. "Yum."

"You're so gross!" Cocoa stomped away.

The boys almost made it to the basement door before Grandma Eunice rolled into their path. Malcolm's great-grandmother had been living with them for as long as he could remember. She was the only one in the family who knew about their ghost detecting.

"What did Dorothy want?" she asked.

"Dorothy?" Malcolm echoed.

"Little Dorothy Twaddle," Grandma Eunice said. "She's Ms. Porter now."

"She has a haunted doll," Malcolm said.

"Or maybe a bunch of haunted dolls," Dandy added.

Grandma Eunice nodded. "She always did love dolls. You boys wait here. I've got something for you that might help." She rolled away toward her room.

Dandy flopped on the floor and rubbed his nose on his sleeve. Malcolm nudged him with his foot. "What are you doing? We have to get our equipment."

"She said to wait here."

"And what if she forgets what we're waiting for?" Malcolm said. "We could sit here all day."

Malcolm knew his great-grandmother wasn't really as forgetful as she acted. She only pretended so his mother wouldn't make her do chores. He thought it was

a pretty smart trick. Too bad he hadn't thought of it.

The squeak of Grandma Eunice's chair made both boys look. She held a bag with the *Ghost Stalkers* logo on it. "I bought this for you at SciCon when we went. I was holding it for your birthday, but it sounds like you need it now."

"Thanks." Malcolm took the bag.

He didn't think they'd need anything from the *Ghost Stalkers*. He used to love their show. But when he met them at SciCon, he wasn't impressed. Still, he didn't want to make Grandma Eunice feel bad so he looked in the bag.

"It's a Poltergeist Popper," she said. "Only $7.99."

She pulled out the Poltergeist Popper. It looked a lot like a spray bottle with some

fancy logo glued on. "Our ghost zapper will do the job. It always does."

"Take the Poltergeist Popper anyway," Grandma Eunice said. "You never know."

"Sure."

But as the boys headed downstairs to get the rest of their equipment, Malcolm was pretty sure he did know. They would have this ghost zapped in no time.

Chapter 4
Giggling Ghosts

Malcolm's mom snagged them on their way back out with the bag of Ghost Detector tools. "How did your visit with Ms. Porter go, boys?"

"It was sweet," Dandy said.

"She wants some help with a home project," Malcolm added. "We're on our way back to do it."

"That's wonderful. I'm glad to see you boys showing so much community spirit."

"We're all about spirit," Malcolm said.

They were almost to the front door when Grandma Eunice rolled into their path. She poked the bag in Malcolm's hand. "Is the Poltergeist Popper in there?"

"It is."

"Maybe I should come with you." Her face looked dreamy. "I loved dolls when I was a girl. I never had as many as Dorothy, but I had a Little Cutie doll and I loved her."

She sighed. "I still miss that doll. I wonder if Dorothy has one. If I came with you, I could look."

"I don't know." Malcolm edged by the chair. "It's a long way to push your chair."

"Think of it as good exercise," Grandma Eunice suggested. She poked Malcolm's arm. "Your muscles could use the building."

"Ow." Malcolm rubbed his poked arm. "Maybe a different time. Besides, you

shouldn't be around Dandy. I think he has a cold. Don't you, Dandy?"

Dandy rubbed at his nose. "It might be allergies."

"Or a cold," Malcolm said. "Besides, Ms. Porter said we have to hurry. So we'll see you later." He finally squeezed around the chair and made it out the door. Dandy squeezed out after him.

"Maybe we should take pictures for Grandma Eunice," Dandy said as they climbed on their bikes. "So she can see the dolls."

"We have to get in and out fast," Malcolm said. "Before word gets around that we're hanging out with Pop Quiz Porter."

When they rolled up to the house of dolls, the front door slowly swung open. "Maybe Porter is still in there," Dandy said.

"Or the ghost is happy to see us," Malcolm said.

"I don't like happy ghosts much."

Dandy backed away from the door. Malcolm grabbed him by the arm and dragged him along. Inside the house, the tumbled mess of dolls was all cleaned up. Every doll was back in its place.

"Looks like the ghost is a neat freak," Malcolm said.

At the sound of his voice, every doll head turned to look at the boys. Even the rocking horse turned to look at them.

Malcolm pulled the specter detector out of the bag and turned it on. He expected to see a ghost turning the doll heads. But all he could see were dolls. He picked up the specter detector and banged it with his hand. No ghost appeared.

"What if the dolls are all really ghosts?" Dandy whispered.

"That's silly," Malcolm said.

But then they heard someone giggle. More giggles joined in. The giggling got louder and louder, all around them. It was as if every doll were giggling.

Dandy slapped his hands over his ears. "Stop laughing!"

The dolls stopped.

Malcolm and Dandy looked at each other. Ghosts didn't usually obey so easily. Dandy took his hands away from his ears. "What do we do next?" Dandy whispered.

Malcolm wasn't sure. If he couldn't make the ghost appear with the specter detector, he couldn't blast it with the ghost zapper. If the dolls followed orders, maybe he could make the ghost show itself.

"Hey," he yelled. "Ghost. Come out and talk to us."

As soon as he spoke, a soft rustle of whispering started. At first, the boys couldn't tell what the whispers said, but as they got louder and louder, it became clear.

"Greedy," the dolls whispered. "Greedy. Greedy. Greedy!"

The whispering turned into angry shrieks. "Greedy! Greedy! Greedy!"

Malcolm and Dandy slapped their hands over their ears. "We should go outside!" Malcolm yelled. "And make a plan."

"What?" Dandy yelled.

"A plan!"

"What?"

Malcolm gave up and ran for the front door with Dandy right at his heels. They almost made it. The front door slammed

shut right in front of them. Then the lock snapped in place.

Malcolm grabbed the door handle and pulled. He tried to turn the lock. Nothing happened. They were locked inside with screaming ghost dolls.

Chapter 5
Blinded By the Light

The screams stopped. The boys looked at each other. "We could try to climb out a window," Dandy suggested.

Malcolm pointed at the nearest window. Two tall dolls stood in front of it with their heads twisted around to stare at the boys. The painted mouths on the dolls slowly turned up into creepy smiles with lots of pointed white teeth.

"I don't think we should get any closer to them," Malcolm said. "We need to

find the ghost and zap it. Then we can go home."

"I really, really want to go home," Dandy whispered. "Soon."

The boys walked through the rooms downstairs. Malcolm held the specter detector, but no ghosts showed up.

All they saw were dolls in every room. Even in the bathroom. A floppy clown doll held a roll of toilet paper and smiled a wide, red smile. "What if there isn't a ghost?" Dandy asked as they stared at the clown.

"Of course there is a ghost. We saw the dolls move."

"Maybe the dolls are evil," Dandy said.

Malcolm had to admit, the clown doll did look a little evil. Still, he shook his head. "There's always a ghost. Let's check upstairs."

On the second floor, dolls perched on every surface except one bed. A huge teddy bear lay sprawled on the doll-printed quilt taking up every inch of space. "That bear is bigger than me," Dandy said.

"At least it's not a doll."

Malcolm walked down the hall to another room full of dolls. When he walked into the room, he heard Dandy sneeze behind him. Then the door slammed shut.

"Hey!" He grabbed the doorknob but it wouldn't turn.

Dandy pounded on the door from the other side. "Let me in."

"Let me out!" Malcolm yelled. Then he remembered. He was a Ghost Detector. He needed to do his job.

Malcolm turned around to face the room of dolls. The biggest doll in the room sat in

a rocking chair. At least none of the dolls were moving.

Malcolm took a careful step closer to the doll in the rocking chair. Maybe he could use the chair to bash the door open. Of course, he would have to touch the doll to do that. He took another step closer and reached out slowly.

He planned to grab the doll's hand and pull it onto the floor really fast. The doll had an open mouth with two teeth. Behind the teeth was just a dark hole in the doll's china head.

Malcolm wondered why a doll maker would leave a hole in a doll's head like that. Anything could crawl into a hole like that. He stepped closer to try to see inside.

Something moved in the darkness of the doll's head. "What is that?"

A big, black spider squeezed out of the doll's mouth. It stood on the doll's red lip, then tumbled off into the doll's lap.

Malcolm jumped back as the spider scurried down the doll's leg and dropped onto the floor. Malcolm tried to stomp the big spider, but it dodged back and forth. Malcolm jumped around and shrieked.

More spiders crawled out of the china doll's mouth. Small spiders poured from the eyes and noses of other dolls around the room. A dark wave of spiders began to spread across the floor.

Malcolm didn't try to stomp the big spider anymore. He just turned and ran.

He hit the door so hard he bounced off, landing on his back near the spiders. He jumped up and pounded on the door. "Let me out! Help!"

On the other side, Dandy rattled the door. It still wouldn't open. "Try the zapper!"

"There's nothing to zap!" Malcolm yelled. "It's spiders, not ghosts."

"Maybe they're ghost spiders!" Dandy yelled back. "Can you see through them?"

Malcolm stomped a few spiders near his shoes. They squished on the floor in a greasy smear. "No, I can't see through them."

He rooted around in the tool bag. *Next time, I'm bringing bug spray.*

With nothing else to try, Malcolm pulled out the Poltergeist Popper.

He pointed it at the spiders and pulled the trigger.

The Poltergeist Popper clicked a few times. Then a white light poured out. It dazzled Malcolm. He blinked and stared around the room, but he couldn't see anything at all. He was blind.

Chapter 6
Teddy Bear, Don't Bite

Malcolm pressed against the door. Now he couldn't even see where the spiders were. He stomped his feet in case they were on the floor.

He wondered if they were already climbing onto his shoes. Maybe they were already on him! With a shriek, he began slapping at his arms and legs.

The door at his back swung open. Malcolm tumbled out onto the floor in the hallway. He scooted back as fast as he could,

slamming into Dandy's legs and knocking him down.

"Look out for the spiders," Malcolm yelled as he crawled over Dandy to get farther from the door.

"Ouch. What spiders?" Dandy asked.

Malcolm pointed toward the room. Or he hoped it was toward the room. He still couldn't see. "In there. There are zillions of them."

Malcolm heard Dandy get up and walk toward the room. "Be careful!" Malcolm said.

"I don't see any spiders." Dandy walked back over and hauled Malcolm to his feet. "The only things in that room are creepy dolls."

"How did you get the door open?" Malcolm asked as he rubbed his eyes.

"I dunno. I saw a bright light from under the door. Then it wasn't stuck anymore."

"The Poltergeist Popper," Malcolm said. "It actually works." Of course, it also made Malcolm blind. He wasn't sure that was a fair trade. He told Dandy what happened. "I think I dropped the popper in there."

"I'll get it," Dandy said.

"Wait." Malcolm hurried over to hold the door open so Dandy didn't get trapped, but he just ran into the wall instead.

"I got it," Dandy said as he walked back into the hall. "There's little bitty print on the bottom of this thing." He read the small print aloud. "Do not use this product without the *Ghost Stalkers* Popper Peepers to protect your eyes. Only $7.99 a pair."

"I wish I knew that before I used it." Malcolm squinted as he looked around

the hallway. He was starting to see a little. Dandy looked like a blob.

Malcolm reached out to grab Dandy's arm but the blob turned out to be a table with a doll on it. Malcolm let it go fast. "Get us out of here."

Dandy pulled Malcolm along behind him. "Everything is quiet now. Maybe the Poltergeist Popper got rid of the ghost. We can go home."

"I can't go home. How do I explain being blind?" Malcolm asked. Dandy accidentally walked him into a wall. Malcolm pulled away. "Don't help me so much."

"Fine," Dandy said, stomping off.

Malcolm rubbed his eyes some more. "Wait a second. I think I can see a little."

He blinked at Dandy. His friend was still fuzzy. In fact, he was really fuzzy.

"Why do you look so funny?" he asked.

"What are you talking about?" Dandy's voice didn't come from the fuzzy blob. "I'm over by the stairs. Come on."

"If you're over by the stairs, what's that?" Malcolm pointed at the fuzzy blob.

He closed his eyes and rubbed them again. When he opened his eyes, the fuzzy blob was much clearer. And it didn't make Malcolm feel any better.

The big teddy bear from the bed stood beside him. The bear roared, ripping open the stitching on its mouth. Piles of white fluff poured out. The bear shook its head, flinging fluff all over.

Malcolm batted at the flying fluff as he backed toward the stairs. He could see a lot better now. He really wished he couldn't. With the fluff gone, Malcolm could see into

the growling bear's mouth. It was a dark hole filled with sharp teeth.

With a roar, the bear charged.

Chapter 7
Men in Black, Jr.

"Run!" Dandy yelled. Malcolm ran. The bear ran right behind him. The bear's big, fluffy paws were slippery on the wood floor. It slipped and slid along. Malcolm made it to the stairs first.

Malcolm climbed on the stair railing. "Slide, Dandy, slide."

"I don't think that's safe," Dandy said. The bear roared again.

Malcolm reached out and dragged Dandy onto the railing. "It's safer than a bear."

They slid down the rail. Dandy yelled the whole way. At the bottom, they tumbled into a pile. Then the bear galloped down the stairs.

Malcolm pushed Dandy off him. "We have to get outside."

Dandy pointed a shaky finger. "The door!"

Malcolm looked. The front door was open, but it was slowly swinging shut. If it closed, would it lock them in with the bear?

He looked back at the stairs. The bear's big, floppy feet weren't made for stairs. It was tripping and bouncing off the railings.

"Use the Poltergeist Popper," Dandy begged.

Malcolm shook his head and ran to the door. "We don't want to be blinded again."

The bear finally tumbled the last half dozen steps and landed in a pile of stuffing and fluff at the bottom. It stood back up, shaking its head and flinging more fluff.

Then it raced after the boys. On the downstairs carpet, the bear was running much faster. They weren't going to beat it to the door.

The door creaked as it swung on its hinges. They had one chance. "Slide, Dandy, slide!" Malcolm yelled.

"I don't know how," Dandy screamed. "I didn't practice."

"Fake it."

Both boys flopped into baseball slides right out the front door and onto the porch. The door bumped Dandy's feet as it finally slammed shut. Dandy and Malcolm grinned at each other. "We made it."

A soft thump slammed into the other side of the door. The bear smushed its face onto the small pane of glass in the door.

They could hear the screech of the bear's teeth on the glass. But it couldn't open the door with its big, fluffy paws. They were safe. The bear couldn't get them.

Dandy and Malcolm ran for their bikes. "We need a new plan," Malcolm said.

"Right," Dandy said. "Let's make the plan at your house."

"I'm good with that."

On the ride home, Malcolm's eyes still stung a little, but he could see again. They needed to figure out a way to use the Poltergeist Popper without blinding themselves.

The more Malcolm thought about it, the more he was sure he had the perfect idea.

When they got to Malcolm's house, they ran inside. "We need Grandma Eunice."

"Maybe she's having a snack," Dandy suggested. "I know I could use a cookie."

"There's no time for cookies," Malcolm said. "This is important. Forget your stomach."

Dandy rubbed his stomach and spoke softly. "Don't worry. I will never forget to feed you."

Grandma Eunice rolled out of the kitchen. "Did I hear someone ask for a snack? I just swiped these from the jar." She held a chocolate chip cookie in each hand. Malcolm decided they had time for a cookie.

While they gobbled the cookies, Malcolm explained their Poltergeist Popper problem. "I think we need some sunglasses."

Grandma Eunice smiled. "I know just what to do. In fact, I think you boys need more than just sunglasses. This sounds like a case for the Men in Black."

"Wasn't that a movie with aliens?" Dandy asked. His eyes widened. "You don't think that bear was an alien?"

"It was a teddy bear," Malcolm said. "I don't think aliens have teddy bears."

"I don't know. It looked pretty alien with all those teeth," Dandy grumbled. Then he took a comforting bite of his cookie.

"We just need glasses," Malcolm said.

Grandma Eunice rolled toward her bedroom. "Tish tosh. Don't argue with me. It's time to suit up, boys."

By the time Grandma Eunice was done, both boys wore dark sunglasses. Malcolm had on the suit his mom made him wear to his cousin Bibi's wedding. Since they didn't have time for Dandy to go home and change, he wore some suit pants Malcolm outgrew and a dance-costume jacket they snuck out of Cocoa's closet.

Dandy brushed at the jacket lapels. "Do the Men in Black wear all this glitter?"

"It's a bold choice," Grandma Eunice said. "But I think you can pull it off."

"It's fine," Malcolm said. "But we have a problem. How do we zap a ghost that never shows its face?"

Chapter 8
Leave Me Alone!

"You'll get it," Grandma Eunice said as she herded them out of her room. "Start with what you do know. The ghost likes dolls. Think about that." Then she rolled back into her bedroom and closed the door.

The two boys stood facing the closed door for a moment, then Dandy gasped. He turned to look at Malcolm with wide eyes. "Ms. Porter really likes dolls. Do you think she's really the ghost?"

Malcolm reached up to knock on Dandy's forehead, making the big sunglasses slide down his friend's nose. "What goes on in there?"

Dandy pushed the sunglasses up on his face. "She's very pale. She could be a ghost."

"Can you see through her?"

"She could be a really thick ghost." When Malcolm reached out to knock on his head again, Dandy jumped back. "Fine! Who do you think likes dolls?"

Malcolm pushed Dandy ahead of him. "Little girls do. I think it's a ghost girl."

"That makes sense, I guess. It's sad though, thinking about a kid ghost."

"But it would explain why she always hides," Malcolm said. "We wouldn't be scared of a little girl. She's been tricking us this whole time. Let's go get that kid."

They hopped on their bikes and raced back to Ms. Porter's house. When they got there, they found the front door open a crack. "Do you think the bear is still in there?" Dandy asked.

"Where would it go?" Malcolm asked.

Dandy shrugged. "To the woods?"

"In our neighborhood?" Malcolm asked.

Malcolm marched up the steps and peeked in through the cracked door. Wads of white fluff lay all over the floor, but he didn't see the bear.

Malcolm walked into the house with Dandy right behind him. In fact, Dandy was so close, he was almost walking in Malcolm's shoes.

"Hey, ghost!" Malcolm yelled, making Dandy jump. "I know you're just a kid like us. You don't scare us."

"It scares me a little," Dandy whispered.

"You might as well come out!" Malcolm yelled.

The front door slammed shut so hard the boys could feel the house shake and hear it groan. A breeze tossed Malcolm's hair. It flapped the front of Dandy's jacket, scattering glitter on the floor.

Then it stopped being a breeze. A wind roared through the room, almost knocking the boys off their feet. The wind swept up the hunks of fluff all over the floor.

The fluff swirled together in a spinning pile. It quickly took the shape of a little girl.

The fluff girl opened her mouth wide, then wider. "I can see clean through her head," Dandy yelled over the roaring wind.

The fluff girl's mouth snapped open and closed. A voice rushed around them in the

wind. "You guessed it. Now get out of my house. Leave me alone."

"No!" Malcolm yelled back. "That's not what Ghost Detectors do."

He reached into his bag and pulled out the ghost zapper. He aimed it at the girl and pulled the trigger. The spray wet down the fluff, making soggy chunks fall onto the floor.

The girl looked down at her dripping fluff hands. She opened her mouth wider than Malcolm's head.

"Leave me alone!" She flung a wad of soggy fluff that smacked Dandy in the head.

"Put on your glasses!" Malcolm yelled as he pulled out the Poltergeist Popper. He hoped Dandy followed directions. The popper blasted the foyer with light. The fluff fell into soggy bits.

59

Malcolm pulled off his glasses. He could still see. "I'm just going to keep popping you!" he yelled. "You might as well show your real self."

"If you insist."

The boys spun around to face the ghostly figure standing in the living room doorway. Dolls spun around her. Malcolm's mouth fell open. The ghost didn't look anything like what he expected.

Chapter 9
It's Mine!

The ghost in the living room wasn't a little girl. It wasn't even a kid.

The ghost woman was older than Grandma Eunice and had twice as many wrinkles. Her eyes looked like raisins pushed into sugar cookie dough. Around her head, white fluffy hair swayed as if in a breeze.

Malcolm dropped the Poltergeist Popper and grabbed the ghost zapper. Should he go ahead and spray her?

"Don't you dare!" The ghost pointed at Malcolm, and the dolls spun around her even faster. "Don't you boys have any manners at all? Zapping and popping little, old ladies. You two ought to be ashamed."

"I kind of am," Dandy whispered.

Malcolm was too, but they had a job to do. They promised to get rid of the ghost. He held up the ghost zapper. The dolls stopped spinning around the ghost and flew at him instead.

"Ow!" Malcolm swatted at the dolls, and the ghost disappeared.

"She sure is fast for an old lady," Dandy said.

"You've got that right, boy-o." The ghost appeared at the bottom of the stairs with her hands on her bony hips. "And I can certainly handle two little boys."

"We're Ghost Detectors," Malcolm snapped as he aimed and sprayed at the ghost. She disappeared before the spray could hit her.

"You're hooligans," the old woman said when she popped into place in the living room again. "If you were nice boys, you wouldn't pick on little, old ladies."

"Us?" Malcolm yelped. "You tried to eat us with a bear!"

She disappeared before he could aim the ghost zapper. "I can't believe two big boys were scared of a sweet teddy bear."

Malcolm spun to see the ghost in the middle of the stairs. "I wasn't scared. I was responding to the situation."

Dandy raised his hand. "I was scared."

"Why are you haunting Pop Quiz Porter's house anyway?" Malcolm asked.

The ghost flung out an arm. "Look at this place. No one needs this many dolls. She's never happy. She always wants more."

Malcolm figured the ghost was right about that. "You don't like dolls?"

"Of course I do. Who doesn't love dolls?"

"I don't like them much," Dandy said.

The ghost held up a bony finger. "I had one doll. My granny gave her to me. She told me to take good care of my Little Cutie. And I did." She pointed at Malcolm. "I always did what my granny said, and you should too."

Malcolm pointed at his friend. "My Grandma Eunice told Dandy to wear that jacket," he said. Dandy sneezed, and glitter rained down around him.

The ghost looked at the glittery jacket. "Fine. Maybe you shouldn't do everything

your granny says. But my granny was special."

"So the doll your granny gave you is here?" Dandy asked.

The ghost nodded. She didn't look angry anymore. She looked sad. "That greedy woman just stuck my doll in with all the others. She didn't love her. She didn't even give her a special spot."

The ghost looked more and more upset. And the breeze picked up in the room again. "That doll is mine!" the ghost shrieked.

"Wait," Malcolm yelled over the roar of the wind. He needed to calm her down before they had a hurricane. "What would we have to do to convince you to leave?"

The ghost glared at him. She crossed her arms over her chest. "I'm not leaving my doll here. She deserves a good home.

Someplace special with someone who loves her as much as I do."

"So you'd leave if we found your doll a good home?" Malcolm asked.

"Maybe." Then she pointed at him. Her arm stretched and stretched until her finger almost touched his nose. "But I'm not giving her to a grubby-fingered child."

"I might have the perfect home," Malcolm said.

"I don't trust you," the ghost said. "I'm not telling you where my Little Cutie is." And with a soft *POP*, the ghost vanished.

"We'll find it anyway!" Malcolm yelled.

The ghost didn't appear, but her voice came at them from all sides. "Good luck with that!"

Then the boys were pelted with rag dolls. They stayed tough until the clown

doll came dancing out of the bathroom. Malcolm and Dandy ran out the front door.

Dandy hung on the porch post and panted. "How are we supposed to find one special doll in there?"

"One special Little Cutie doll." Malcolm smiled at his friend. "And I know exactly how to find it."

Chapter 10
Pop Her!

"Wait here!" Grandma Eunice said as soon as Malcolm told her what they needed. She rolled back into her room.

Malcolm and Dandy flopped down on the couch to wait for her. On the television, a lady was telling them about a cream for getting rid of toe hair.

Dandy pushed off one sneaker to look at his toes. "Do you have hair on your toes?"

"No," Malcolm said. "Put your shoe on. We need to be ready to go."

"You sure?" Dandy asked. "Maybe you should check. That lady on the television says it's a problem."

"I don't have toe hair."

Dandy hopped up and tried to pull off one of Malcolm's shoes. They wrestled for a while until finally Grandma Eunice rolled back into the room. "What are you boys doing?"

"Checking for toe hair," Dandy said.

Grandma Eunice nodded. "I have that problem. I can loan you some cream later."

"Forget the toe hair!" Malcolm said.

He stood up and dusted off his suit. Then he noticed Grandma Eunice's clothes. She was wearing a pantsuit and dark sunglasses.

When she saw Malcolm looking, she grinned. "Let's go bust some ghosts."

Malcolm almost told her she was mixing up movies. But he decided to save his breath for pushing her wheelchair. Once outside, the boys pushed Grandma Eunice to Ms. Porter's house.

When they got there, Malcolm was gasping and Dandy was panting. "You two need more exercise," Grandma Eunice said. "You're a little noodle legged. Let's go, boys!"

Still panting, Malcolm and Dandy pushed the wheelchair to the bottom of the porch stairs. Dandy flopped over into the grass. "Just a second," he gasped. "Need to breathe."

"Yeah," Malcolm agreed. "Hold on. We'll haul you up the stairs."

He looked at the stairs, then he looked at his grandmother. He had no idea how they

were going to haul her up the four steps to the front porch.

"Don't be silly," Grandma Eunice said. "I would squash you boys like a bug." She stood and walked slowly up the steps. At the top, she turned and smiled down at them. "Now you can bring the chair."

After a lot of tugging and bumping and gasping, Malcolm and Dandy hauled the chair onto the porch. Grandma Eunice patted each boy on the head and sat back down in the chair. She wiggled into the best position then pointed at the front door. "Charge!"

When Grandma Eunice rolled into the living room, she gasped. "There are a lot of dolls in here."

"Are any of them Little Cutie?" Malcolm asked.

"Give me a minute," she said.

Grandma Eunice opened one of the stuffed glass cabinets. Dolls tumbled into her lap and she looked them over. "Not this one. Not this one." With each wrong choice, she dropped the doll into one of the baskets.

Dandy flopped down on the floor to wait. Malcolm walked around the living room with the ghost zapper in his hands. Suddenly, he felt a cool breeze.

"Uh, Grandma Eunice, maybe you should look faster," Malcolm said.

"What's your hurry?" she asked.

Grandma Eunice turned her chair just as the rocking horse came to life and snapped at her. She grabbed a newspaper from the coffee table, rolled it up, and smacked the horse on the nose.

The horse snapped again, grabbing the newspaper and chewing it to bits. Dandy scrambled to his feet as Grandma Eunice slipped on her shades. "You better pop them, boys."

Malcolm shoved on his own sunglasses and rooted in the bag of gear. He grabbed the Poltergeist Popper and pulled the lever. It didn't click. It didn't light up. It fell apart in his hands.

The rocking horse galloped over. Then it gobbled up the fallen pieces.

Grandma Eunice smacked at the horse with another newspaper. "I tell you. $7.99 doesn't buy what it used to."

The horse snapped at Malcolm.

He shoved the last piece of Poltergeist Popper handle into its mouth. The horse tried to munch, but the handle was too big.

"Gotcha!" he said.

Malcolm was feeling pretty good until he saw every doll in the room twitch a little. "Oh, no."

He grabbed the ghost zapper.

The china dolls lurched to their feet. The rag dolls flopped out of their baskets to crawl along the floor. Two rag dolls wrapped around Dandy's ankles.

"Malcolm!" Dandy yelled.

Malcolm started toward his friend. Troll dolls jumped off a shelf and onto his head, pulling his hair and giggling. Malcolm swatted at the trolls. Dandy kicked and punched rag dolls. And then Grandma Eunice screamed.

Everyone froze. Grandma Eunice didn't sound scared. She sounded happy. Really happy.

She scooped up one of the dolls from the floor and began hugging it. "A Little Cutie," she cooed. "Just like I always wanted."

When she said this, the dolls tumbled over in a quiet heap. Dandy untwisted a troll from his hair and tossed it to the floor. "Are you sure that's a Little Cutie?"

The ghost appeared. "Of course it is." She drifted over to Grandma Eunice. "Do you really like her?"

Grandma Eunice nodded. Her eyes sparkled. "I always wanted one."

"You'll take care of her?" the ghost asked.

"The best care in the world."

The ghost looked at her for a long moment. Grandma Eunice just hugged the doll and smiled. Finally, the ghost smiled too. "I can leave her with you. But don't

let anything happen to her. Somewhere, Granny is watching."

And with that, the ghost disappeared.

Grandma Eunice hugged the Little Cutie doll as Malcolm and Dandy slowly pushed her home. "I hope Pop Quiz Porter

doesn't mind losing one doll," Dandy huffed.

"I don't know how she would notice," Malcolm puffed.

"I'm sure she'll feel like it's worth it to get her house back," Grandma Eunice said. "You can call her when we get home."

"I don't know her number," Malcolm wheezed.

"I do," Grandma Eunice said. "I can make the call. Maybe Dorothy and I could go doll hunting together sometime. I could buy some friends for my Little Cutie."

Malcolm stopped pushing. "Do you think that's a good idea? Buying dolls is what started this problem."

"Tish tosh," Grandma Eunice said. "You know what? The three of us make a good team. We should work together more often."

Malcolm and Dandy looked at each other. That was the scariest thing they had heard all day!

Malcolm started pushing again. "We better get you home."

"Right away," Dandy agreed.

As they rolled up to Malcolm's door, Cocoa walked out. She pointed at Dandy. "That's my jacket! I'm going to kill both of you!" She stormed down the stairs at them.

Malcolm and Dandy let go of the wheelchair and ran. As they ran, Dandy turned to him. "I don't think we're going to need that training course."

Malcolm had to agree. Having the family he had was the best training a Ghost Detector ever needed.

Questions for You

From Ghost Detectors
Malcolm and Dandy

Dandy: I was glad I didn't see the ghost spiders. Spiders are scary. And ladybugs. I'm creeped out by ladybugs. What creatures scare you? What do you do about it?

Malcolm: Cocoa was really mad about her jacket. Have you ever got in trouble for borrowing something without asking? What did you do? I could use some tips.

Dandy: Ms. Porter's dolls were super creepy, but I think collecting is cool. If you could collect anything in the world, what would you collect?

Malcolm: I think my training course is really going to help us be better Ghost Detectors. Do you have anything you want to get better at? What are you doing to make that happen?